SPACE SCOUT™

SCOUTING THE UNIVERSE FOR A NEW EARTH

The Shrinking Race
published in 2010 by
Hardie Grant Egmont
85 High Street
Prahran, Victoria 3181, Australia
www.hardiegrantegmont.com.au

The text for this book has been printed on ENVI Carbon Neutral Paper.

A CiP record for this title is available from the National Library of Australia

Cover illustration by D. Mackie
Illustrated by C. Bennett
Design by S. Swingler
Typeset by Ektavo
Printed in Australia by McPherson's Printing Group

1 3 5 7 9 10 8 6 4 2

THE SHRINKING RACE

BY H. BADGER
ILLUSTRATED BY C. BENNETT

hardie grant EGMONT

Kip Kirby sat at his school desk, swinging his legs.

He was meant to be taking a Health and Nutrition test, like the other 999 kids in his class. But Kip's mind was elsewhere.

He was thinking about his after-school job. It wasn't an easy one, like being an

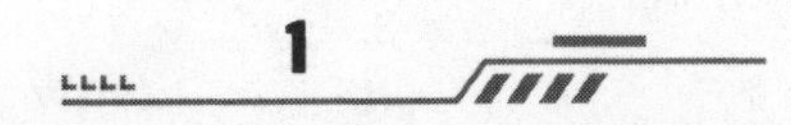

ePaper Boy. That just meant uploading the morning paper into the electronic slot in people's front doors.

Kip's job was way harder, but heaps more fun. He had been specially chosen by the massive corporation WorldCorp to be a Space Scout.

Earth was so crowded that it was running out of room. Another Earth was needed – fast! It was the Space Scouts' job to find it. So Kip got to explore unknown planets beyond the Milky Way in a high-tech black starship.

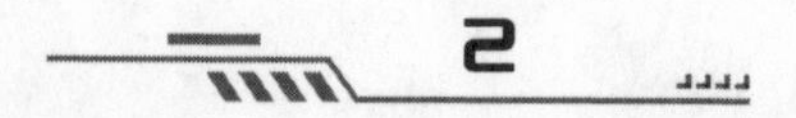

Kip glanced at his school desk. It was a new Thoughtomatic. The test questions flashed onto the desk's built-in screen:

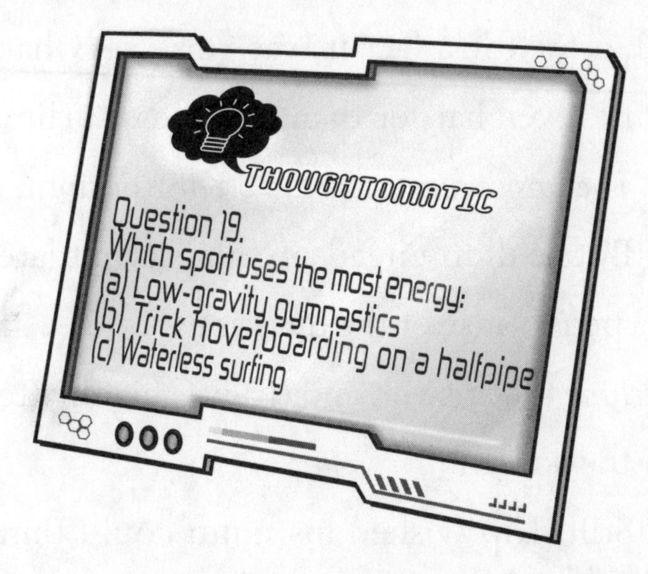

Kip sometimes watched low-gravity sports comps broadcast live from Mercury.

Those low-gravity gymnastics are easy-peasy. Humans weigh 62% less on Mercury, Kip remembered. After his time in Space

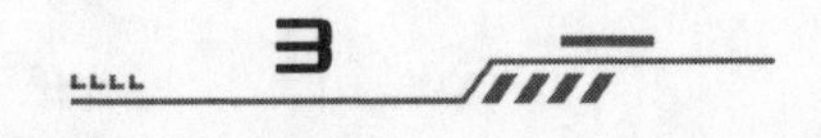

Scout training, Kip's space knowledge was impressive.

Also, Kip was an expert hoverboarder. He knew for a fact it was very, very hard work, even harder than waterless surfing.

The answer's got to be (b), Kip thought.

But he didn't need anything as outdated as a pen to answer the question. Kip just had to *think* the answer, and (b) was highlighted on the screen.

Still, Kip wished his mum could think his answers for him. She was a Health and Nutrition whiz. It seemed like it, anyway. She was always telling Kip to eat his artificial vegies.

Kip knew that in the olden days, vegies

were grown on farms. Now everything was created in labs.

Kip had read in his history downloads that kids had never liked vegies. But now vegies tasted worse than ever – just like the fluff in his spacesuit cuffs!

The next question flashed up on the Thoughtomatic screen:

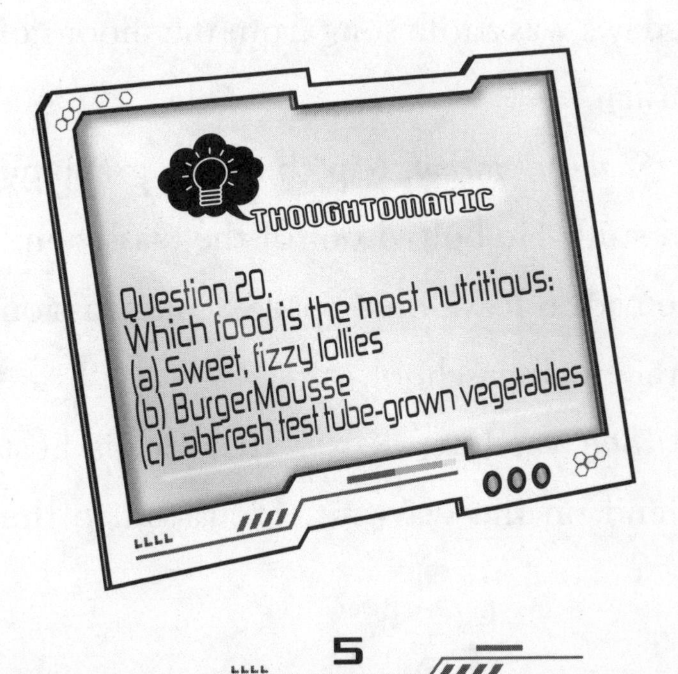

BurgerMousse was Kip's favourite snack. It was yummiest when sprayed out of the can straight into your mouth. According to Kip's mum, BurgerMousse was definitely unhealthy. So were lollies.

The answer's got to be (c), Kip thought, just as the bell rang. The bell was polyphonic, and it played a different tune every day. Today's was a folk song from the moons of Saturn.

Soooooo uncool, Kip thought, grabbing his stuff. He bolted out of the classroom. He had to leave on a Space Scout mission straight after school.

'See ya, Jett,' Kip yelled to his best friend on the way out. He raced to the school gate, which was made of invisible lasers. He cleared it in a single jump.

Where's my UniTaxi? Kip wondered, scanning the street. All he could see were Nannybots. These robots picked up kids after school and looked after them while their parents were at work.

When Kip needed to travel to the Intergalatic Hoverport, WorldCorp often sent a UniTaxi. UniTaxis were flying vehicles used for high-speed travel within Earth's atmosphere.

When Kip wasn't on a mission, his starship docked at the Hoverport, about 10 kilometres off the ground. His starship was called MoNa 4000.

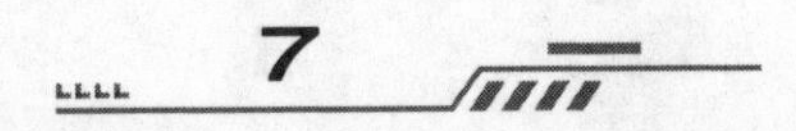

Better call WorldCorp and find out where the taxi is, Kip thought to himself. He flicked on his SpaceCuff. SpaceCuffs were thick silver wristbands with mini screens. Space Scouts used them to talk with WorldCorp and their starships when on missions.

There was already a message waiting on Kip's SpaceCuff.

'Inconvenient? They're risking Earth's future!' Kip snorted. 'Hopeless.'

Kip grabbed his custom-made World-Corp spacesuit, which was rolled up in his school backpack. The spacesuit was bright green and made of extra strong meteor-repellent fabric.

He jammed on his green spaceboots, the latest Humming-bird Pros. His matching helmet had glittering flames on the side.

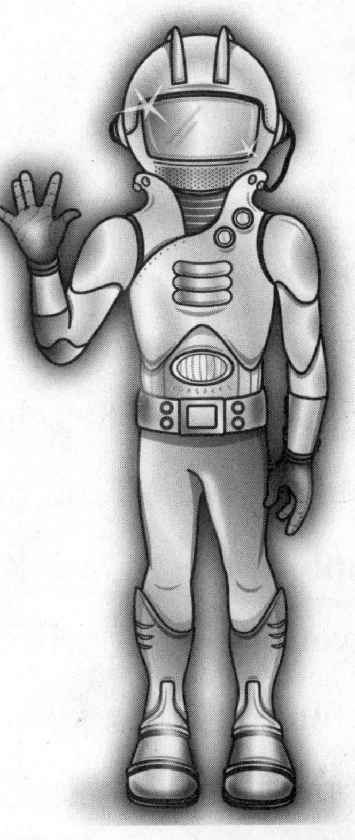

Kip would have to find his own way to the Hoverport!

Kip raced towards the school's shelter sheds. They were silver waterproof pods at the back of the school.

He scanned the shelter sheds for Jett's Junior Flyer. It was Kip's old one. Kip had given it to Jett when he became a Space Scout. A Junior Flyer just didn't compare to piloting MoNa 4000.

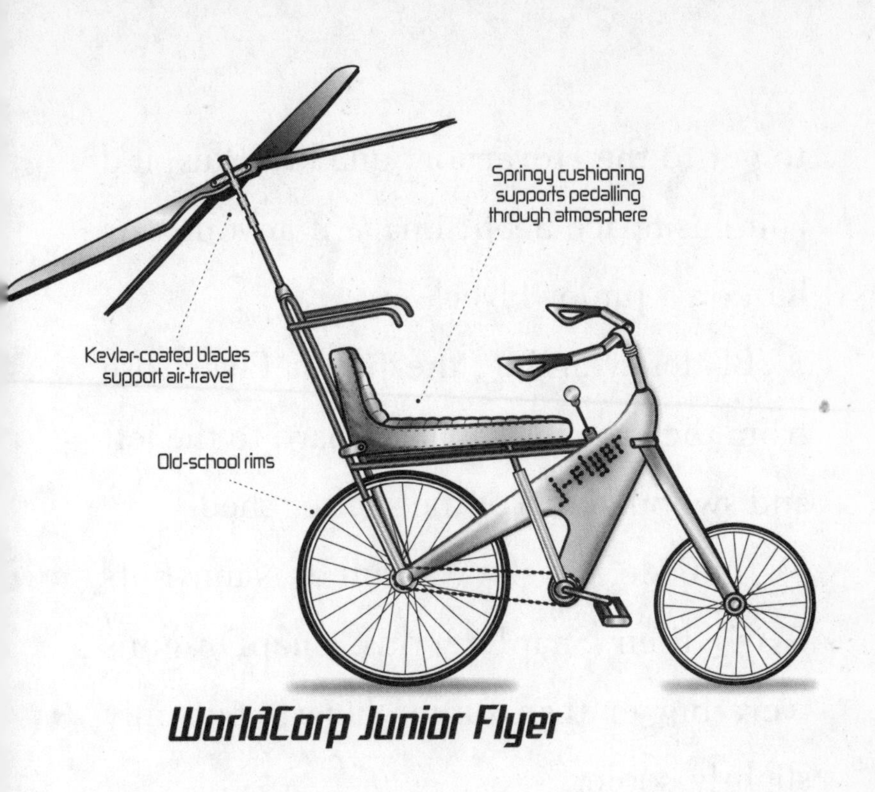

WorldCorp Junior Flyer

Hope he doesn't mind if I borrow it back! Kip thought, jumping on.

Junior Flyers had two wheels and a carbon-fibre frame. The helicopter blades behind the seat were pedal-powered.

Kip started pedalling like crazy. He had

to get to the Hoverport quickly. Plus, it'd ruin his Space Scout image if anyone saw him on a Junior Flyer!

Blades whirring, the Junior Flyer rose from the ground. Kip leant hard to the left and swooped out of the shelter shed.

Outside, the sky was full of Nannybots flying their SnapDragons. SnapDragons were bigger than Junior Flyers, but only slightly cooler.

Kip flew higher, dodging the traffic with skill. The wind was picking up. It nearly blew him straight into a Nannybot!

He was panting so hard that his helmet fogged up. Luckily, Kip was ultra-fit. To make it as a Space Scout, he had to be.

At last, the Hoverport loomed up ahead. The Hoverport looked like a multi-storey carpark hovering in mid-air. Starships of all shapes and sizes were docked there. Most were small spacecraft that didn't fly further than Neptune's icy asteroid belt.

Only bigger starships like MoNa could explore deep space beyond the Milky Way. MoNa was a glossy black starship with curved thrusters and glowing lights underneath.

Arriving at the Hoverport on a Junior Flyer, Kip cringed. *MoNa will never let me live this down!*

MoNa thought Kip was too young to be a Space Scout. After all, at 12, he was

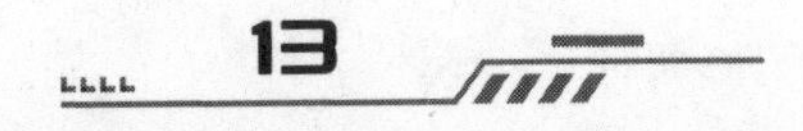

the youngest of the 50 Space Scouts. And MoNa loved teasing him.

Kip took a sharp left and pulled up outside MoNa's landing bay. He tapped the Communicate button on his SpaceCuff. 'Kip Kirby to MoNa 4000,' he puffed. 'Lower the landing bay door.'

'Is that you, Kip?' laughed MoNa's computerised voice. 'I thought it was the ePaper Boy. Must be that Junior Flyer you're on.'

'Very funny, MoNa,' Kip muttered as the landing bay door lowered.

Kip zoomed into the landing bay and screeched to a stop. The landing bay was a huge, empty grey space on MoNa's lowest level. He pulled off his helmet and wiped his sweaty face with his spacesuit sleeve.

The main landing bay door closed with a sucking, hissing noise. At the other end, an airlock opened. Kip's second-in-command Finbar stepped through.

Finbar was part-human, part-arctic wolf. He walked on his hind legs and stood two metres tall. Finbar was an Animaul, a creature that'd been specially cross-bred to protect Earth in case aliens invaded.

'What's up, Fin?' asked Kip. 'Er, are you OK?'

Normally, Finbar's fur was soft and pure white. But today he looked all sweaty and grubby. 'WorldCorp installed a MagnaSweep,' Finbar replied. 'I've been run off my paws guarding it.'

When not on missions, Finbar lived on MoNa and kept her safe. But playing guard-wolf wasn't his favourite part of the job.

Finbar became Kip's second-in-command (or 2iC for short) after failing Animaul training for being too gentle. His intelligence made him an awesome 2iC, even if he wasn't as brave as Kip. Plus, he had a wolf's super vision and hearing.

'The MagnaSweep's magnetic field is impressive,' Finbar continued eagerly.

'It sweeps space debris for metal and clears it before it can get stuck in MoNa's thrusters.'

'Enough chit-chat,' MoNa cut in crisply. She heard everything Kip and Finbar said.

'She's been grumpy since we heard the rumour,' Finbar whispered in Kip's ear.

'What rumour?' Kip asked. The Space Scout intranet constantly buzzed with gossip.

MoNa jumped in. 'Everyone's saying that another Space Scout's discovered Earth 2.'

A jealous flush rose on Kip's cheeks. Someone else was about to win the Shield of Honour?

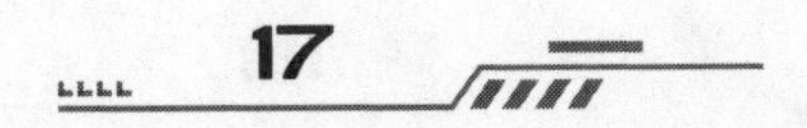

WorldCorp ranked Space Scouts on the Planetary Points Leader Board. After each successful mission, Space Scouts earned one Planetary Point. Two were awarded for a promising discovery.

The Space Scout who discovered Earth 2 would win the ultimate prize – the Shield of Honour.

Kip wanted to win the shield more than anything. Partly for the glory, but also for the prizes. The successful Space Scout would be given a mansion on the new Earth, with the latest StarFlight Personal Transportation Module in the garage!

It's just a rumour, Kip told himself. *There's no way I'm giving up on that shield yet.*

The rumour had shaken Kip. But one of his best Space Scout talents was bouncing back. Now he was extra-determined to get on with his mission.

In silence, Kip and Finbar strode to the bridge to download their mission brief. The bridge was MoNa's command centre, located in her nose cone.

At the door, Kip's eyeball was scanned with a security laser.

Inside, the bridge had huge windows looking out over Earth. The entire floor was a lit-up map of the known universe. In the centre were two padded chairs.

Kip sat down and waved his hand in the air above his head. Instantly, a cylinder of blue light shot down from the roof. The light surrounded Kip and Finbar's chairs.

Complicated dials, buttons and screens were projected onto the light. This was Kip's holographic consol.

MoNa had a useful auto-pilot mode. But Kip's piloting skills were vital, too. He was an expert at flying. He had an unbelievable ability to concentrate on heaps of things at once.

Kip touched a holographic button that said Download Mission Brief. The brief appeared, projected in mid-air.

CLASSIFIED

WorldCorp's telescope has discovered a new galaxy in the universe's Far West Quarter.

Scientists calculate a wormhole is opening soon. It leads to a blue planet named Cobalt. Nothing is known about the planet, except that it is nearly the same size as Earth.

Kip's stomach flipped. A little while ago, a Space Scout called Candy Montenegro had made a promising discovery in the Far West Quarter. Now Kip had a chance to explore a new planet nearby!

'Depart Hoverport for wormhole to Cobalt,' Kip commanded MoNa.

'Look out the window, genius,' sniffed MoNa.

Kip had been busy reading the mission. He hadn't noticed MoNa was on auto-pilot. She'd left the Hoverport and guided them into deep space.

Focus, Kip, he told himself irritably. *This isn't the way to beat that other Space Scout.*

'There's the wormhole,' said Finbar,

pointing to a mass of blue cloud up ahead.

A wormhole was a shortcut from one galaxy to another. Using wormholes, Space Scouts could travel billions of light years in seconds.

Kip snapped into professional Space Scout mode. Taking MoNa's controls, Kip steered them to the wormhole. MoNa was sucked inside instantly.

Kip's skin prickled. His eyes throbbed in their sockets. Travelling faster than the speed of light was tough.

'Rogue asteroid heading this way!' yelled Finbar suddenly.

A massive craggy rock whizzed towards MoNa's left window. If it hit the window, the air pressure in the bridge would change radically. MoNa could explode!

'Engage Anti-Matter Cannon,' Kip commanded. He was trained to stay cool under pressure. At once, MoNa's Anti-Matter Cannon rose up from her roof.

Kip pressed the Fire button. Faster than light speed, the Anti-Matter Cannon shot hot pink plasma at the rock. The plasma stream smashed into the rock and vaporised it. There was nothing left but mist.

A second later, MoNa popped out the other end of the wormhole. Kip took a deep breath and leant back in his chair.

'There's Cobalt,' MoNa said, clicking back to auto-pilot as though nothing had happened.

Through the windows, Kip spotted a blue, Earth-sized planet. It was orbiting around a single sun, just like Earth. One side was sunlit. The other was in darkness.

Kip and Finbar jumped up and headed back to the landing bay. There, Scrambler Beams would send their particles through space and rearrange them on Cobalt.

Kip and Finbar put on their helmets. They checked their gloves and spaceboots were sealed to their spacesuits. The air on Cobalt might not be breathable, so they carried compact air-supplies called OxyGlobes on their backs.

Finbar took ages to get ready. Kip knew that the Scrambler Beam made him space-sick. Kip practically had to drag his 2iC to the pair of pawprints marked on the landing bay floor.

Kip stood next to him as two beams of light shot down from the roof. Before Finbar had time to whimper, their scrambled particles went shooting through deep space.

Kip felt all tingly. Being reformed was a bit like having pins and needles all over your body! Scrambling was a seriously weird experience.

Kip found himself lying on the ground. He sat up.

Quickly, Kip flicked his SpaceCuff to Air-Analyser Mode.

Air-Analyser Mode:

67% Oxygen

32% Nitrogen

1 % Sugar Particles

WARNING: Local plant-life releases sugar particles into the air. In human noses, these tickly particles may cause snotty sneezes.

Kip figured that if humans lived on Cobalt, they'd need to breathe with OxyGlobes the whole time. The sneezing would be too annoying and gross, otherwise.

Not perfect, Kip thought. *But it doesn't mean we couldn't live here.* After all, people took holidays to Venus all the time. Humans couldn't breathe there either.

Kip captured some air in a pressurised

test tube. WorldCorp's scientists could confirm the analysis later. Kip stashed the tube in his backpack as Finbar appeared next to him.

Before flicking off his SpaceCuff, Kip noticed a message.

But Kip didn't have time right then to wonder why Candy was at HQ. He wanted to get a feel for Cobalt.

Arriving on a new planet was Kip's

favourite part of Space Scouting. He was the first human ever to see the blue, grassy field in front of him. In neat rows along the fields were bushes with oddly-shaped fruits hanging from the spindly branches.

Gleaming silver buildings stood around the field. The buildings didn't seem to have any windows or doors.

Next to Kip, Finbar groaned as his particles slotted back into place. He picked himself up just as Kip spotted something.

A blue figure stood nearby, trimming the strange bushes. Kip's Space Scout training had taught him to notice every detail.

The figure was about 15 centimetres tall. He was human-like with blue skin and

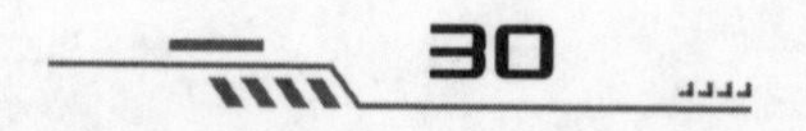

pale blue hair. He wore coloured shorts and a matching singlet.

The aliens of Cobalt are so small! Kip thought. *Humans could easily share their planet if they agree.*

'Let's introduce ourselves,' whispered Kip to Finbar.

'Greetings!' Finbar said to the tiny blue man. 'We're from planet Earth.'

The blue man looked up in fright. Then he dived under the nearest bush!

'I bet we look like freaky giants!' Kip whispered.

'We're not going to hurt you,' Finbar politely told the blue man.

Kip hoped that Finbar's calm tone

would reassure the blue man. But still the man didn't come out.

'Let's give him a present to show we're friendly,' Kip suggested to Finbar.

In his backpack, Kip had just what he needed to impress an alien. Chocanos!

Chocanos were the best lolly in any known galaxy. They were candy-coated and shaped like tiny volcanos. As you sucked, the centre erupted through the candy. You ended up with a mouthful of warm melted chocolate.

Kip walked towards the bush, an unwrapped Chocano in his hand. 'Please, take it,' Kip said, super-friendly.

He pointed to his mouth to show the

gift could be eaten.

The blue man peeked out of the bush. Cautiously, he crept towards Kip.

With both hands, the blue man heaved the Chocano off Kip's hand. It was a quarter of the size of the blue man's head. He opened his mouth wide. He could only just fit the Chocano in!

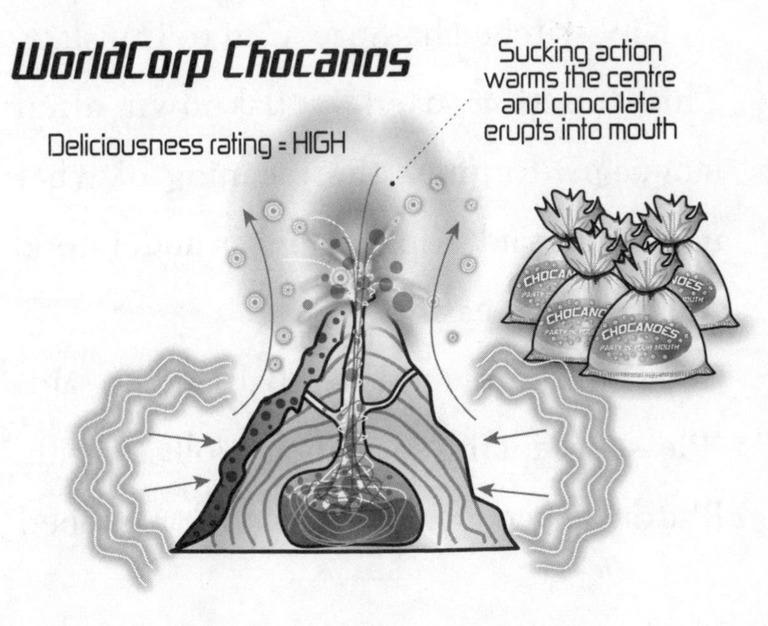

The blue man sucked. Warm chocolate dribbled from his mouth. His eyes crinkled with pleasure.

The blue man held out his tiny hand. Kip shook it with his fingertip.

No-one can resist a Chocano! Kip smiled.

The blue man began talking. His soft voice was strangely powerful.

Kip switched his SpaceCuff to Translate. This function used well-known alien languages to guess the meaning of what new aliens said. Kip and Finbar understood the blue man easily.

'I'm Blutor, and I'm a Baltian,' he said. 'Please accept this sugarmelon lolly as a gift.' Blutor picked a bright pink melon-shaped fruit from a nearby bush.

In Kip's hands, the melon was tinier than a gumball. He popped it into his mouth using the special airlocked compartment in his helmet. Flavour exploded on his tongue. His mouth filled with fizzy pink juice. The lolly was thousands of times sweeter and more delicious than a Chocano!

'Mmmm!' said Kip. He had an instant craving for another sugarmelon.

When Blutor handed him some more, Kip wanted to eat them all at once. He forced himself to save one as a sample for WorldCorp's scientists.

'You love sugarmelons as much as we do,' smiled Blutor. 'Our scientists first

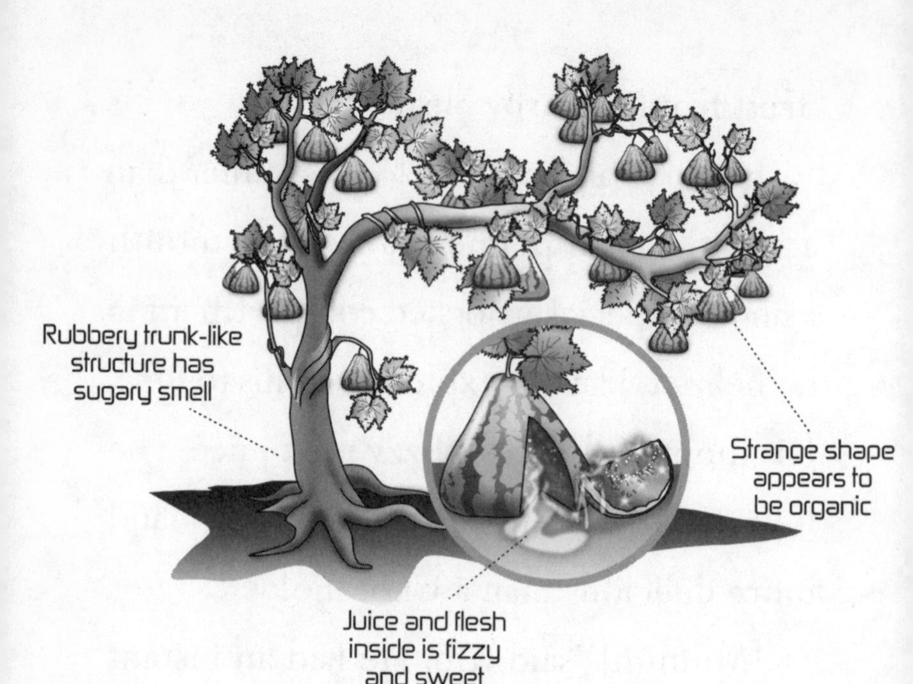

grew them on trees about two years ago. Now, no-one eats anything else.'

If I lived here, I'd pick lollies off the trees all day long, Kip sighed to himself. *Much yummier than LabFresh vegies.*

Finbar tried a sugarmelon. Kip could

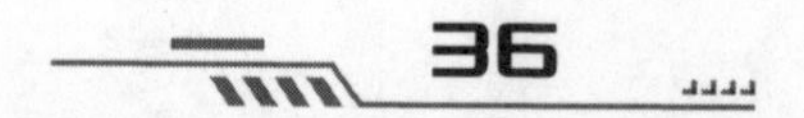

tell Finbar didn't like the lolly, even though he was trying to be polite. Because he was part-wolf, Finbar didn't have a sweet tooth.

'Hope they've got good dentists,' Finbar whispered to Kip.

But Kip wasn't going to ask Blutor about dentists. They seemed to be making friends. *Maybe now's the time to tell Blutor about our mission,* he thought.

Kip didn't have time to explain anything to Blutor, though. At that moment, a figure rushed towards them. She looked like Blutor, except she was younger and had long pale blue hair.

'There's been another accident!' puffed the little blue girl. 'Someone has fallen down a drain.'

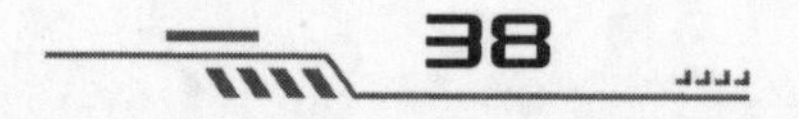

‘They’re smart enough to grow lollies on trees,’ Finbar whispered to Kip. ‘So why would they build drains big enough for someone to fall down?’

Kip shrugged. Finbar had a point.

‘Our ropes aren’t long enough,’ the blue girl added.

‘We’ll help!’ said Kip.

Cobalt could be Earth 2, Kip thought. *If we save the day, Blutor and his people might share their planet in return.*

Plus, Kip was trained to always help friendly aliens in distress.

‘That’s our city, Cobaltville,’ said Blutor. He nodded at the silver buildings around the field.

'I'll carry you there,' said Finbar, scooping up Blutor and the blue girl. 'We'll get to the accident faster that way.'

Kip and Finbar raced across the sugar-melon field and into Cobaltville.

The red-paved streets were crowded with blue people talking about the accident. Everywhere, digital signs flashed updates. A tiny blue dog-like animal with horns yapped at Kip's heels.

More and more Baltians ran out of the silver buildings. The buildings had no doors, though. The walls looked like they were *melting* to let the people walk through them. Then they formed again, as though they were made of liquid-metal. It looked

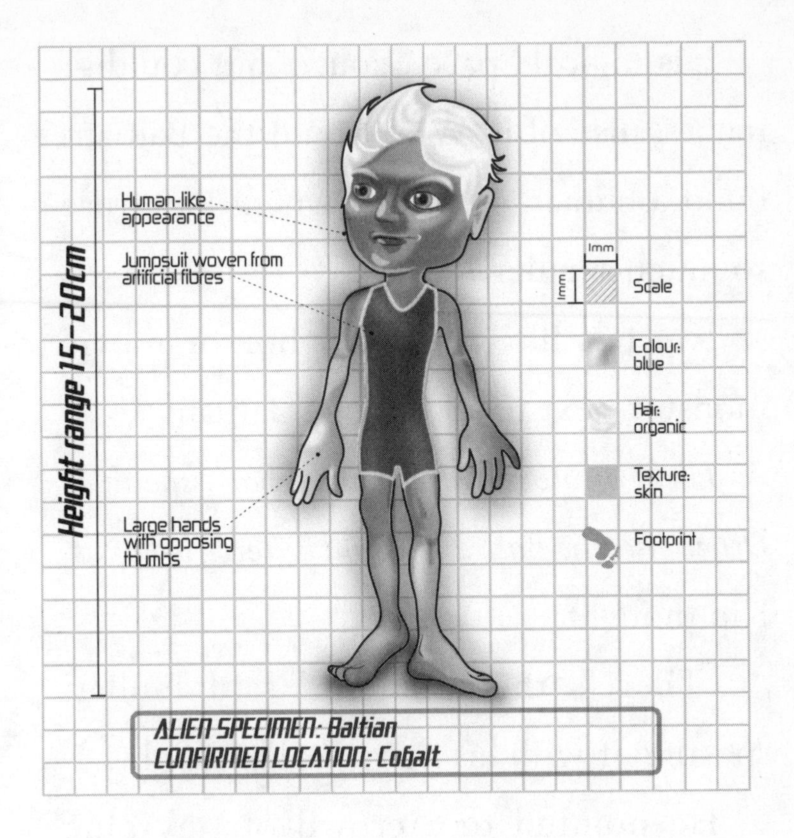

a bit like walking through a waterfall.

Kip made a quick mental measurement of the buildings. They were the perfect height for humans. Not Baltians.

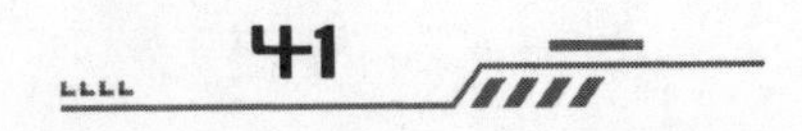

His logical Space Scout brain couldn't make sense of it. Why would the Baltians build a human-sized city when they were so much smaller?

Kip felt like a gigantic horror-movie monster next to all the tiny Baltians.

Lucky Blutor's riding on Finbar's shoulder. Otherwise, the Baltians would be terrified of us, Kip thought.

'There's the accident,' said Finbar, spotting it with his sharp wolf eyesight.

He pointed to a crowd of tiny blue figures gathered around an open drain. The drain hole was no wider than Kip's backpack. But to the tiny Baltians, it was a bottomless pit.

Finbar gently put down Blutor and the little blue girl.

'Fellow Baltians,' Blutor said. 'Our Earthling friends are here to help with the rescue.' The crowd erupted in cheers and clapping.

Cobalt's hopes are riding on us, thought Kip. *As if finding a new planet for Earth wasn't enough!*

Kip mentally ran through the contents of his backpack. He had safety gear like ropes and harnesses with him, of course. But the ropes would be too big for the Baltian to grab a hold of.

As he thought about what to do, Kip spun the glowing meteorite chip he wore

around his neck. It hung from a chain made of extra-strength carbon fibre.

Kip was a master at making do with what he had. He prided himself on coming up with solutions on the spot, even when he didn't have the right gear.

With his gloved hands, Kip unclipped the chain around his neck and slipped the chip into his pocket.

He bent close to the drain. *It doesn't look too deep*, Kip thought. *Hopefully this chain will be long enough to reach the bottom.*

Kip knelt. The nearby Baltians scattered away from Kip's giant feet.

Slowly, he fed the chain into the drain.

A crowd gathered, munching on

sugarmelons. They watched as Kip fed the entire chain down the drain.

Doubt crept into Kip's mind. Would the chain be long enough? Could the Baltian take hold of the end?

He waited. Nothing.

Back in Space Scout training, Kip topped the class in Crisis Handling. The most important thing he learnt was:

The worst thing I can do now is doubt myself, he decided. *I'll never beat the other Space*

Scouts to the Shield of Honour that way.

Just then, Kip felt something tug on the chain! But it was so soft that Kip wondered if he'd imagined it.

'I'll pull you up,' Kip whispered. He didn't want to scare the Baltian down the drain with his booming voice.

Gently, Kip pulled up the chain.

The crowd watched. Everyone held their breath.

Kip knew they were all thinking the same thing.

Will the missing Baltian be hanging on the other end?

Kip pulled the chain out of the drain. And clinging tightly to it was the missing Baltian!

Kip held out a finger. The Baltian grabbed on. Carefully, Kip put the tiny blue boy down on the ground.

As Kip stood up, he saw two blue people run over to the muddy Baltian. They hugged him, crying.

That must be his mum and dad, Kip thought. *Funny to think that even little blue aliens have parents.*

On the edge of the crowd, Blutor signalled to Finbar to lift him up.

Blutor spoke gravely to Kip and Finbar. 'If only all rescue missions were this successful,' he said, shaking his head. 'We've lost too many people to accidents.'

Kip paused, wondering how to answer. Blutor and his people were obviously smart. Kip didn't want to offend them.

'Have you thought of building smaller drains?' Kip asked politely.

'Our problem is more difficult than

drains,' Blutor said sadly.

Kip shot a glance at Finbar. Neither knew what might come next.

'Over the last two years,' Blutor went on, 'our people have shrunk from your height to the size we are now.'

'What?' Kip said, shocked. 'How?'

He'd heard about all kinds of strange planets from other Space Scouts. But no-one had ever mentioned a shrinking alien race!

'We cannot explain it,' said Blutor, rubbing his blue chin.

He's worried about the future of his people, Kip thought. *Just like I'm worried about the future of Earth.*

At that moment, the sound of grinding metal pierced the air.

ER-RRRRRRRRRR!

It sounded like a rusty starship changing gears.

'Put me down!' Blutor said quickly. 'We must hide!'

Blutor and the other Baltians disappeared through their silver walls. Within seconds, the city was deserted.

ER-RRRRRRRRRR!

'It's getting louder!' yelled Finbar, covering his ears. 'Run!'

Kip thought ahead for a moment. It was a vital Space Scout skill. *If we run into the buildings, we might crush a Baltian*, he thought. *Then they'll never want to share their planet with us.*

It was a risk Kip couldn't take. They had to find somewhere else to hide.

'The sugarmelon field!' Kip yelled.

'Look!' said Finbar, as they ran. He'd spotted a green shape in the sky. It was heading straight for them!

The shape got closer. Kip saw it had a beak and giant wings.

'That's too heavy to be a bird,' Finbar said. 'See how it swoops when it's flying?'

'It's metal,' Kip yelled, noticing the creature's body glinting in the sun. 'It's some kind of winged robot!'

The robot circled directly overhead.

Its screech was ear-splitting and there were dagger-sharp claws on its feet.

Kip dragged Finbar towards him. Flicking on his SpaceCuff, Kip engaged the InstaShield mode. Lines of powerful electrical currents sprang from the Space-Cuff and arced above Kip and Finbar.

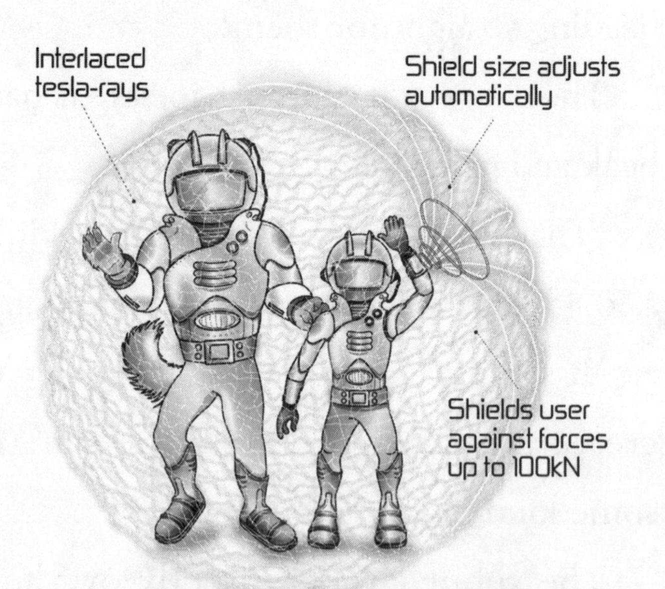

SpaceCuff InstaShield Mode

In nanoseconds, they were safe inside a bubble of electrical mesh. Just in time!

The winged robot dived down. It slammed into the electrical bubble. Sparks exploded.

ZZZZTT!!!

A burnt metallic smell filled the air. The winged robot crowed miserably. It flew off, spewing smoke.

When the sky was clear, Kip switched off the InstaShield. Across the field, the Baltians reappeared through their liquid-metal walls.

'That's your second rescue in one day,' said a voice behind them. It was Blutor.

'What *was* that thing?' Kip asked him.

'An Aerobot. When we were big, we built them to hunt small creatures known as steak mice,' Blutor explained. 'And we farmed vegetables ourselves.'

'You stopped hunting and farming when the sugarmelon craze hit,' Finbar guessed.

A troubled look crossed Kip's face. 'And when your people began to shrink, the Aerobots started hunting you!'

Blutor nodded. 'We needed to reprogram them,' he said. 'But we couldn't. Our people are simply too small.'

Unstoppable flying attack-robots. It sounded like a nightmare!

Kip's mind turned all this over. If Cobalt was going to be Earth 2, he would have to find a way to deprogram the Aerobots.

Before he could work out how, something hit his helmet with a crack.

Colours exploded around Kip's head. He guessed what was happening. MoNa had fired him a NewsBomb!

A NewsBomb was a small, round ball with compressed news data inside. It broke open on impact, releasing a 3D holographic broadcast from Earth. It was like standing inside a TV.

Back on Earth, WorldCorp had called a Space Scout meeting for all those not on missions.

Now Kip found himself standing inside a live a holographic version of the meeting!

Space Scout meetings almost never happen, Kip thought. *What's going on?*

A holographic WorldCorp rep was talking. 'Attention, Space Scouts! You've probably heard about Candy Montenegro's promising discovery in the Far West Quarter. WorldCorp's scientists have nearly finished studying her plant samples from the Crimson Planet. Nothing is confirmed, but signs indicate that Candy has discovered Earth 2.'

The hologram faded, leaving Kip white-faced.

Finbar came over, still holding Blutor.

'Nothing's final,' Finbar reminded Kip. 'You can't give up until you see the shield in Candy's hands.'

Finbar was right. Until that happened, there was still a chance…

Kip put Candy out of his mind and focused on the Baltians' problem. 'Deprogramming the Aerobots is the next step,' he said. 'Wiping their memories is the quickest way.'

Back on Earth, robots had memory failure all the time. Their circuits overloaded, or sometimes they just wore out.

An idea nagged at Kip. Something he'd heard back in Space Scout training...

'Siberian robots wear out more often than others,' he said, thinking aloud.

Blutor and Finbar stared at Kip. It was a bizarre time to be babbling about Siberian robots!

'The Earth's magnetic field is very strong in Siberia,' Kip continued. 'WorldCorp's scientists think the magnetic field wipes the robot's memories!'

Kip turned to Blutor with a grin. 'I happen to know of a very powerful magnet that might do just that for you.'

'MoNa's new MagnaSweep!' said Finbar. 'Brilliant idea.'

Kip looked down at his SpaceCuff. He tapped out a message.

There was a split-second pause. Then Kip's SpaceCuff buzzed furiously.

She's right, Kip thought. He hated it

when that happened.

But Kip now knew his deprogramming plan wouldn't work without this important piece of information.

'Where do the Aerobots live, Blutor?' asked Kip at once.

'When the Aerobots grew powerful, they moved out of Cobaltville,' Blutor said grimly. 'We don't know exactly where they live now. And our people have grown too afraid to leave the safety of the city.'

Kip could see that Blutor hated how weak the Aerobots had made the Baltians. Finbar gave Blutor an understanding smile.

'There are rumours the Aerobots have settled in the Badlands,' Blutor went on.

'The Badlands?' Kip asked.

'The unexplored territory on the dark side of Cobalt,' Blutor said. He explained that a Baltian day was hundreds of Earth years long.

'Which means the other side is totally dark,' finished Finbar.

Kip asked Blutor if he had information about getting to the Badlands.

'They're on the other side of Shifting Flat,' said Blutor. 'It's north of here.'

Kip flicked his SpaceCuff to Compass mode. He turned until the digital needle pointed north.

'Ready?' asked Finbar, trying to sound cheerful.

Kip knew Finbar wasn't looking forward to meeting those screeching Aerobots again. But they had to get on with the scouting mission.

'Let's go,' Kip said.

Finbar put Blutor down. He waved Kip and Finbar goodbye. They turned, crossed the sugarmelon field and left the city behind them.

Venturing into unexplored territory on an alien planet. Hunting for powerful winged robots in the darkness.

It sounded incredibly dangerous.

But Kip knew it was what he and Finbar had to do. For the sake of Earth's future – and Cobalt's!

Outside the city, the sandy ground was bright blue. Lush sugarmelon bushes grew everywhere. Kip couldn't resist picking more sugarmelons.

But the further from the city they went, the fewer sugarmelon bushes they found. Soon, all Kip saw were dead plants.

He guessed that the plants would have

once been fresh vegetables. Now they were brown and wilted.

Hiking to the Badlands will take ages, Kip realised. He had heaps of energy from the sugarmelons, but Finbar didn't like them. For Finbar, the trek would be a struggle.

Time to test our new Hummingbird Pros! Kip decided, reaching down to his boots.

The back of each pair of Hummingbird Pros was fitted with tiny, flexible wings. They ran on rechargeable batteries in the boots' sole. The batteries would not stay charged forever. But they'd get Kip and Finbar some of the way at least.

At the touch of a button, the wings popped out. Suddenly Kip and Finbar were lifted a few centimetres off the ground. The boots' wings buzzed loudly and Kip and Finbar took off at top speed. They glided along like mid-air rollerbladers.

Soon, Kip noticed Cobalt's sun dipping low in the sky. The sky faded to black. They were nearing the dark side of Cobalt.

When their Hummingbird Pro batteries

were flat, Kip and Finbar touched down. Blue sand stretched out in every direction. It was like a huge, blue desert.

On the gloomy horizon, Kip could just make out some twisted rock formations.

'Think this is the Shifting Flat?' Kip asked.

But Finbar just stood staring at his feet. 'Feel that?' he said softly.

'What?' asked Kip.

Suddenly, a jet of sand shot a hundred metres straight out of the ground. It looked like water shooting out of a whale's blowhole.

'THAT!' Finbar yelled.

The sand jet finished spraying. Then

another one shot up, millimetres from Kip's feet. Suddenly, sand jets were exploding all over the place.

'Run!' said Kip. 'Head for the rocks!'

They bolted. Sand jets sprayed up and then disappeared until the gloomy air was thick with stinging blue sand.

Kip weaved around the sand jets as best he could. It was impossible to tell where the next jet would shoot up!

'Look out!' Kip yelled to Finbar. The sand behind Finbar had started to shift.

Too late! The sand jet shot into the air. It took Finbar with it, high into the sky. Finbar was in mid-air, surfing on sand!

That almost looks fun, Kip thought,

despite the danger Finbar was in.

Without warning, the sand jet dropped down again. Finbar smacked into the ground. He got up and kept running.

'There are some rock formations to our left,' Finbar panted. His wolf eyes were reliable, even in the low light. 'The Shifting Flat finishes there, I think.'

Relieved, Kip and Finbar raced to the rocks. They collapsed behind the nearest one. The ground underneath them was rocky and solid.

Some blue sand had got into Kip's helmet through the airlock. But he didn't want to take his helmet off to shake it out.

I'm not risking snotty sneezing in the Baltian

air, he thought. *That'd be way too gross.*

His eyes were adjusting to the gloom. He looked around at the rock formations.

Lots of nooks and crannies, Kip thought. *The perfect spot for Aerobots...*

With Finbar leading, they picked their way between the rocks. They stayed absolutely quiet. The slightest sound could alert the Aerobots that they were there.

Suddenly, Finbar stopped walking. In the darkness, Kip almost ran into him.

With one paw to his helmet, Finbar reminded Kip to be quiet. He pointed.

Finbar had spotted an Aerobot! It was sheltering in the darkness of a rocky crevice. It stood there, perfectly still, and

a row of lights blinked softly on its metal chest.

Kip scanned the rocks in front of him. Now he knew what he was looking for, he spotted Aerobots everywhere. There were hundreds of them. No, thousands!

Resting. Waiting.

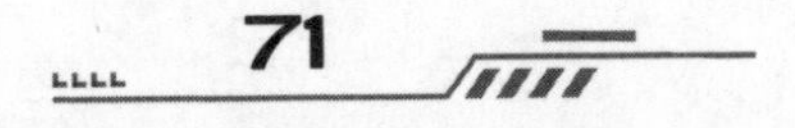

Inside Kip's helmet, a grain of sand flicked up into his left nostril.

His nose began to tickle.

Ignore it, he told himself sternly.

But the tickle built. And built. Soon, it was a ferocious itch.

Don't you dare sneeze, Kip Kirby, he thought. But...

AAAAAAAAA-CHO!

Too late!

A huge sneeze rattled Kip's helmet.

That was all it took to wake up the Aerobots.

Metal wings stirred and beat the air furiously. Terrible screeches filled the night. The Aerobots were about to attack!

Hot with fear, Kip dialled MoNa on his SpaceCuff.

'Engage MagnaSweep 169 kilometres north of Cobaltville, on the dark side of the planet,' he yelled.

Aerobot screeches filled his ears.

For once, MoNa didn't make any jokes. She knew the situation was deadly serious.

'I've got a lock on your location,' she said. 'Engaging MagnaSweep now.'

The Aerobots' wings sounded like swords clashing against their metal bodies.

Kip felt a steely claw scrape the back of his spacesuit.

The claw closed around his shoulder and Kip's feet lifted off the ground. An Aerobot had him in its clutches! It was trying to fly off with him.

'Nooooooooooo!' howled Finbar.

Then suddenly, the Aerobots' screeching stopped. Their wings fell silent and still.

The Aerobot let go of Kip. He dropped to the ground, and commando-rolled to a stop.

The other Aerobots started dropping from the sky too. They landed with a loud clanging of metal, and then sat perfectly still on the ground. A gentle electronic hum filled the air. It was the sound of robots in stand-by mode.

HUMMMMMMM

'It worked!' grinned Kip, getting up. 'MoNa's MagnaSweep's magnetic field wiped their memories.'

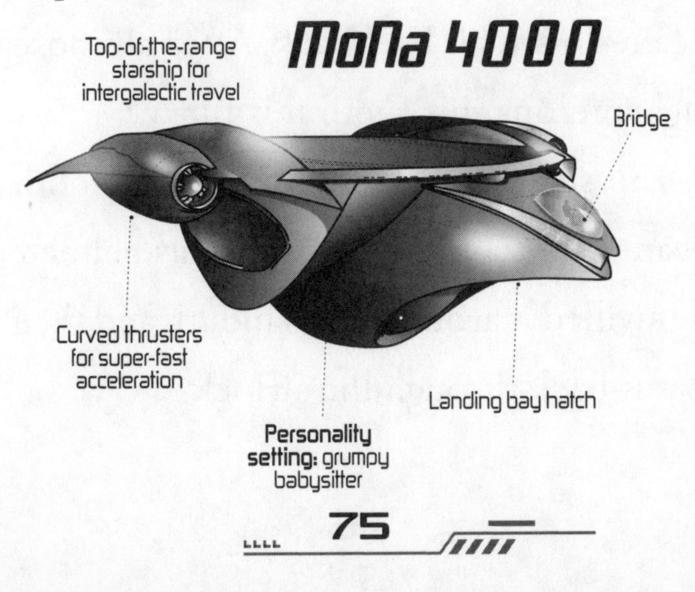

'Let's trek back to Cobaltville and share the good news,' Finbar said.

Kip's gaze settled on a nearby Aerobot. 'Why walk?' he asked, a smile spreading across his face. 'We've got winged robots at our service.'

Finbar looked doubtful.

'Don't be boring,' said Kip, giving Finbar a friendly punch on the shoulder.

Kip cracked open a can of liquid teeth cleaner from his backpack. After all those sugarmelons, his teeth felt furry.

Kip sucked up the entire can of tooth cleaner through the airlock in his helmet. He swilled it around in his mouth and then spat it back through the airlock.

Then Kip and Finbar sat on the back of an Aerobot. Kip programmed Cobaltville's co-ordinates into the robot's computer.

The Aerobot flapped its powerful wings and lifted off. Twisting and turning, it weaved through the rock formations easily. It rose even higher, soaring on each gust of wind.

'You were right,' said Finbar, holding Kip around the waist. 'This *is* better than trekking!'

But Kip wasn't listening. He was thinking about sugarmelons. His teeth felt better after being cleaned, but his tummy ached from all the sugar.

Kip wouldn't have admitted it to his

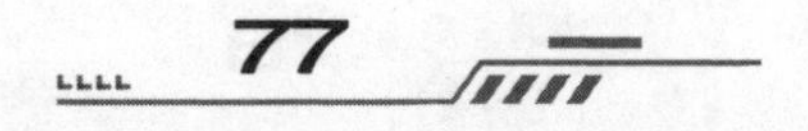

mum or even a Teacherbot, but he felt like he'd had enough lollies for a week!

'The Baltians live on lollies. They don't eat vegies or anything healthy,' he suddenly called over his shoulder to Finbar, thinking aloud.

Far below them, Cobaltville was coming into view.

'Their diet's not nutritious. Maybe that's why they're shrinking!' Kip went on.

He was sure his theory was right.

Blutor said the shrinking began two years ago. That's when sugarmelons were invented!

The Aerobot touched down in the field in the middle of Cobaltville. When the Baltians caught sight of the Aerobot, they ran for cover.

Just in time, Finbar spotted Blutor. 'It's OK!' Finbar called. 'We've deprogrammed the Aerobots!'

'It's safe to come out!' Blutor yelled to the other blue people.

Blutor ran over to Kip and Finbar as quickly as his little legs could carry him.

'I think I know why you're shrinking, too,' Kip said, when Blutor got closer.

Can't believe I'm about to give a lecture about healthy eating! Kip thought.

'Maybe it's your diet,' he suggested.

'You aren't getting any nutrients from fresh vegetables.'

'Lollies growing on trees,' Blutor said slowly, shaking his head. 'I knew there had to be a downside.'

The streets of Cobaltville were filling up with tiny blue people. Everyone wanted to clap and cheer for Kip and Finbar.

So this is how it feels to be a hero, thought Kip. He desperately wanted to beat Candy to the shield and be a hero on Earth too.

But deep down, Kip knew Cobalt wasn't the new Earth he was looking for. The Baltians weren't ready for planet-mates just yet.

After all, it could take the Baltians

years to grow back to their normal size. And they'd have to regrow their vegetable farms, and get back into hunting steak mice – whatever *those* were.

But what if Kip told WorldCorp exactly what Cobalt was like? He couldn't be sure that WorldCorp would agree that the people of Cobalt needed time.

But if I do tell WorldCorp about Cobalt, it might mean winning the shield...

Help the Baltians? Or try to win the shield? Kip had never faced such a difficult choice.

'I'd better call for our Scrambler Beams,' Kip said to Finbar. He didn't want to leave the cheering crowd. But he couldn't put off his decision forever.

'Send two Scramblers,' Kip said into his SpaceCuff.

'Send two Scramblers, *please*,' replied MoNa.

She wouldn't boss me around if I'd discovered Earth 2, Kip thought. Then he realised that probably wasn't true.

Actually, no matter how important I become, MoNa WOULD still boss me around.

The thought made Kip smile.

MoNa was waiting out of sight, in Cobalt's atmosphere. She shot down a pair of Scrambler Beams.

Finbar carefully picked up Blutor one final time.

'It won't be easy for the blue people to grow back to normal size,' Finbar said to Blutor. 'But I know you'll get there if you eat your vegies!'

Blutor shook Finbar's paw goodbye.

Kip didn't really know how to say goodbye.

'My mum makes a really healthy cauliflower casserole,' he blurted out. 'I'll send you the recipe.'

What am I talking about? Kip wondered. *I HATE cauliflower casserole!*

Blutor shook Kip's pointer finger. With a final wave, Kip and Finbar each stepped into a Scrambler Beam. Kip noticed that his 2iC had his eyes squeezed shut.

Finbar might have been a gigantic human-cross-arctic wolf, but he was totally soft when it came to space travel.

Moments later, Kip was sprawled on the floor of MoNa's landing bay. Finbar

was already there, whiskers trembling.

'Let's head straight to the bridge,' Kip said quietly to Finbar. 'I've made my decision. We can't tell WorldCorp that Cobalt could be Earth 2. It's not fair to Blutor and his people.'

Finbar looked at Kip and nodded. He seemed relieved.

Kip and Finbar strode to the bridge. Kip was dreading news of Candy's victory. But his heart told him he'd made the right choice.

Kip engaged the holographic console.

The very first post on the Space Scout Intranet was about Candy!

Kip speed-read through it.

UPDATE

Candy Montenegro's Crimson Planet discovery

WorldCorp's scientists discovered that Candy Montenegro's plant and flower samples had a delicious chocolate smell. But the flowers contained deadly bacteria. Three days' exposure can cause madness and death. Therefore the quest for Earth 2 continues.

END MESSAGE

'Yes!' he muttered under his breath.

Immediately, Kip felt guilty. He *did* want Earth 2 to be discovered. He just wanted to be the Space Scout to do it. And now there was still a chance that could happen. But Kip also needed to protect the people of Cobalt.

His fingers skipped over the holographic keyboard as he filed his mission report.

CAPTAIN'S LOG
Cobalt

CLASSIFIED

Locals: Friendly blue people who are shrinking faster than my granny. Also a fleet of intelligent winged robots called Aerobots. Useful to humans, but only when they're doing what they're told.

Diet: Baltians have the sweetest tooth of any known alien species. They hate vegetables even more than I do.

Recommendation: Cobalt is not the next Earth. Half the planet is almost always in darkness.

Plus, there are no vegetables to eat. Normally I'd say that sounds like paradise. But this mission has changed my mind.

KIP KIRBY, SPACE SCOUT #50

Not totally true, Kip admitted to himself. *But I'm not lying either.*

While Kip was typing, Finbar unpacked a LunchPod he found in the bridge.

LunchPods were lightweight, portable metal ovens. You put the ingredients in and then the LunchPod cooked your lunch.

'Your mum packed us a picnic,' said Finbar.

'What is it?' said Kip. After nothing but sugarmelons for the entire mission, he was starving.

Maybe it's a Mega Meaty Big N Cheesy pizza ice-cream! he thought, drooling.

'There's a massive steak for me,' said Finbar, and then he paused. 'And, er, a cauliflower casserole for you.'

Kip rolled his eyes.

'But she packed dessert too,' Finbar added.

Kip's eyes lit up.

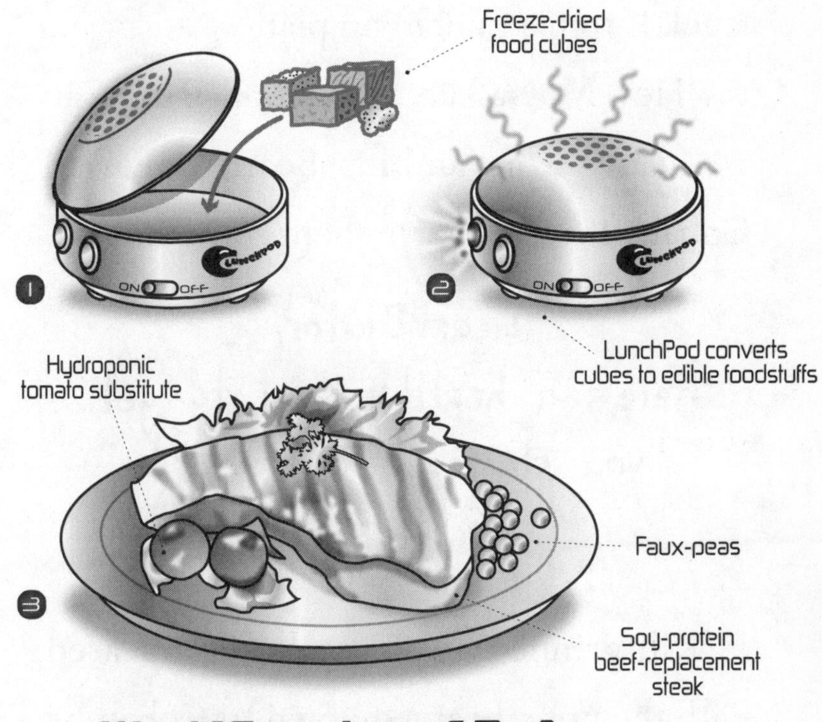

'Sweet Brussel Sprout Pops,' Finbar finished. He made a strange sound, somewhere between a bark and a laugh.

Suddenly Kip had an idea. He scribbled something down on a slip of paper and stuck it to his LunchPod plate.

'Hey, MoNa,' he said with a grin. 'Can you send a Scrambler Beam down to Cobalt? I want to give them something.'

Dear Blutor,
Here's a healthy meal to get you started. Good luck!
From Kip

Kip grinned as his lunch disappeared with the note, beamed down to Cobalt by

MoNa. His mum would never know.

Besides, he thought, *the Baltians need it way more than I do.*

And luckily, Kip had a snack-sized can of BurgerMousse in his backpack for emergencies!

THE END